Amelia Bedelia

☼ Sets Sail ⚓

Amelia Bedelia

Sets Sail

WITHDRAWN

by Herman Parish

pictures by Lynne Avril

me ♥

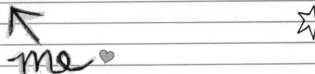

Greenwillow Books

An Imprint of HarperCollins Publishers

Library of Congress Cataloging-in-Publication Data
Parish, Herman.
Amelia Bedelia sets sail / by Herman Parish ; pictures by Lynne Avril.
pages cm.—(Amelia Bedelia ; #7) "Greenwillow Books."
Summary: "Amelia Bedelia and her mother share a summer vacation home at the shore with her aunt Mary
and her cousin Jason, who has a wicked sense of adventure and a nose for trouble"—Provided by publisher.
ISBN 978-0-06-233405-3 (hardback)—ISBN 978-0-06-233404-6 (pbk. ed.)
[1. Beaches—Fiction. 2. Family life—Fiction. 3. Friendship—Fiction. 4. Humorous stories.]
I. Avril, Lynne, (date) illustrator. II. Title.
PZ7.P2185Arb 2015 [Fic]—dc23 2014050045
15 16 17 18 19 CG/RRDH 10 9 8 7 6 5 4 3 2   First Edition

Greenwillow Books

For Stan Parish,

always *Down the Shore*—H. P.

For Laura and Craig—you went above

and beyond. Thank you!—L. A.

Contents

Chapter 1

Causeway? 'Cause Why?

Amelia Bedelia pinched herself. She was so excited, she felt as though she was levitating! They were on their way to the beach!

She looked out the car window. She was sure that if she took a running jump across the bay, she could land in the soft beach sand and run

1

the rest of the way to Aunt Mary's house.

Amelia Bedelia adored her aunt. Aunt Mary always gave the best presents and was good to others and herself. She wore the most stylish clothes and hairdos. She loved jewelry, especially rings, and her nails were always polished—usually with really cool designs. And her son, Jason, was the best cousin ever.

But as soon as Amelia Bedelia's dad drove onto the bridge that went out to the shore, their vacation came to a screeching halt.

2

"Bumper-to-bumper traffic," he said, slamming on the brakes.

"Looks like lots of people love the beach as much as we do," said Amelia Bedelia's mother.

"This is a long bridge," said Amelia Bedelia as they inched along.

"It's not that long," said her father.

"This bridge will take a long time to cross," she said, sighing.

"You know, this bridge is really a causeway," said her father.

"'Cause why?" asked Amelia Bedelia.

"Not why," said her father. "Way. Causeway."

"'Cause it takes way too long?" asked Amelia Bedelia.

"No," said her father. "'Cause it's the only way to the beach."

Amelia Bedelia's mother rolled her eyes and shook her head. "Instead of taking his word for it, why don't you look it up in the dictionary?"

"'Cause why?" asked Amelia Bedelia's father.

"*Because* you make stuff up at every turn, left and right!" said Amelia Bedelia's mother.

"Mom, we can't turn left or right," said Amelia Bedelia. "'Cause we're stuck

on this bridge. I mean, causeway."

"That's my daughter," said her father, glancing back at Amelia Bedelia in the rearview mirror. Then he reached over and patted Amelia Bedelia's mother. "Maybe you should have married a no-nonsense engineer."

"I'm glad you didn't, Mom," said Amelia Bedelia. "Even if Dad was an engineer, we'd still have to drive. The train doesn't go to the beach." Amelia Bedelia looked out at the bay. There were several

small islands covered with trees. She spied a cottage on one of the islands. Now *that* would be a relaxing place for a vacation, she thought. No bridge. No causeway. You could only get there by boat. You'd even have to go to the grocery store by boat!

They rose higher and higher in the air as the car crept along. Finally they were in the middle of the bridge part of the causeway. Boats passed under them. The traffic stopped again. Amelia Bedelia's father sighed and shut his eyes for a second.

BAAAAAAAAHHHNNN!!!

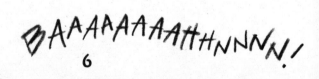

BAAAAAAAAHHNNN!

6

"Who's honking at me?" yelled Amelia Bedelia's father.

Amelia Bedelia saw a fishing boat down below, motoring under the bridge.

"It was that boat, Dad," she said.

"Well, we're almost there," he said, steering the car off the causeway.

"Here at last," announced Amelia Bedelia's mother. "Look at that!"

She pointed to a beautiful small sailing ship on display in the town square. It was flying a pirate flag.

"Do actual pirates vacation here?" asked Amelia Bedelia.

"Maybe in days gone by," said

her mother. "But not today."

As they turned onto Beach Avenue, they each took in a long, deep breath of the salty air. People wearing swimsuits and shorts and flip-flops were walking along the sidewalks. There were kids eating ice-cream cones and other kids with kites and boogie boards. If someone wanted to relax and take it easy, this looked like the place to do that.

"Can we move here?" asked Amelia Bedelia. "It's so relaxing and . . ."

Suddenly her father made a sharp turn into the driveway of a pale blue house.

"Gracious," said Amelia Bedelia's mother. "Mary painted her house! Good

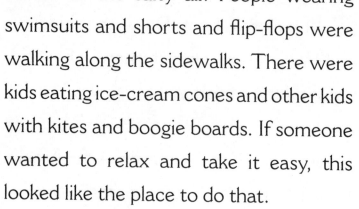

thing you recognized it, honey."

Before they could get out of the car, the screen door on the porch banged open. Amelia Bedelia's cousin Jason took a flying leap off the top step and landed in the soft sand next to their car. He yanked the car door open and pulled Amelia Bedelia out of her seat.

They began jumping and dancing around together in a wild circle until they both tripped and fell down, laughing.

"Finally!" Jason said, putting his

skull-and-crossbones ball cap back on his head. "What took you so long?"

Aunt Mary came outside and hugged everyone. "Welcome!" she said. "We should all be dancing in circles. The weather is going to be spectacular this week!"

"Don't tell me that," said Amelia Bedelia's father. "Turns out I have to drive home on Monday morning and work all week. But I'll be back next weekend."

"Then there's no time to lose," said Aunt Mary. "Let's hit the beach!"

"Absolutely," said Amelia Bedelia's mother. "We can't wait."

Amelia Bedelia started taking off her clothes, right there in the driveway.

"Amelia Bedelia!" said her father.

"What are you doing?" said her mother.

"Don't worry," said Amelia Bedelia, whipping off her T-shirt. "I'll be in my birthday suit in two seconds!"

Chapter 2

Happy Birthday Suit

Two seconds later, Amelia Bedelia's clothes lay in a heap at her feet.

Striking a pose, she turned in a circle and sang out, "Ta-dah!"

Amelia Bedelia's parents and her aunt Mary looked stunned.

"What are you guys stressing about?" asked Jason.

"She's wearing a bathing suit, duh."

Amelia Bedelia was wearing a really pretty black-and-white bathing suit. The grown-ups breathed sighs of relief.

"I didn't want to waste any time changing," said Amelia Bedelia. "So I wore my suit under my clothes." Turning around to model it, she said, "Remember, Aunt Mary? You sent it for my birthday. This is the first chance I've had to wear it."

Ta-dah!

"That's right!" said Aunt Mary, laughing. "That is one cute birthday suit, if I do say so myself!"

Amelia Bedelia was all set for the beach, but now her parents had to get ready.

"Let's get moving," said Amelia Bedelia's father. "Where are my trunks?"

"In the car," said Amelia Bedelia's mother. "Your trunks are in the trunk."

Aunt Mary showed them to their room, so they could get changed. Jason took Amelia Bedelia to his room and gave her the bottom bunk. After she'd dumped her bag on the bed and admired the view of the beach out the window, he said, "Come on, I've got skimboards!"

"No swimming until we get there, young lady!" called Amelia Bedelia's mother as Amelia Bedelia

and Jason clattered out of the house.

Amelia Bedelia and Jason each grabbed a board from the porch and raced over the grassy dune and down to the beach.

"Okay, Amelia Bedelia," yelled Jason. "Start running!"

They began running side by side at the very edge of the waves, where the water was super shallow and the sand was smooth and wet.

"Now throw the board down in front of you," yelled Jason, "and then hop on."

They both threw down their boards.

Jason jumped on with both feet and skimmed along the beach. Amelia Bedelia hopped on her board with one foot—THUD—and she went nowhere. Jason skimmed back to Amelia Bedelia.

"What happened?" he asked. "Just

watch me and do what I do."

She did, and this time she went skimming ahead of Jason. "Wahhhhoooooo!" *Wahhhhooooooo!* she yelled.

Amelia Bedelia's parents appeared over the dune. Amelia Bedelia's father started sprinting toward the surf, yelling, "Last one in is a rotten egg!"

Dashing right past Amelia Bedelia, he accidentally stepped on her skimboard and went whizzing toward a large wave.

"Yee-ayyy!" he bellowed, just barely balancing on the speck of speeding board. He threw up his hands and shut his eyes as the board took a sharp turn, flying along the beach on the crest of the wave. He sailed into the air and crash-landed on an enormous clump of soft seaweed, sunny-side up.

"You were terrific, honey," said Amelia Bedelia's mother. "Are you okay?"

"I've never seen anything like it," said Aunt Mary. "Except on the blooper shows."

"I've had enough ocean for today," said Amelia Bedelia's father.

"Good choice," said Amelia Bedelia. "You're better off being a rotten egg than a scrambled one."

Aunt Mary opened a giant umbrella and spread a beach blanket under it,

in the shade. Amelia Bedelia's father slumped down next to the cooler and sighed, "At last!"

"We're going to take a stroll and catch some rays," said Aunt Mary as she and Amelia Bedelia's mother began walking toward the jetty.

"As long as they aren't stingrays," warned Amelia Bedelia's father.

"We'll be fine," said Aunt Mary. "Stay here and catch some z's."

"I'll join you in a jiffy," he said.

Amelia Bedelia and Jason decided to follow their mothers. Amelia Bedelia actually wanted to stay and help her father. Catching z's sounded like more fun.

"Can you surf too?" asked Amelia Bedelia as they walked along. There were some real surfers riding the bigger waves just off the beach.

"I don't have a surfboard," said Jason. "But we can always bodysurf."

Amelia Bedelia shook her head. "Maybe I could stand on your back and ride you, but I don't think you can stand on me. I'd sink."

"No," said Jason, skipping a rock across the water. "People don't ride you like a surfboard. Your body is the board, but *you* ride the wave in to the beach. I'll show you—come on!"

Jason and Amelia Bedelia swam out to where the surfers sat astride their boards, bobbing on the swells and waiting for the perfect wave. When the next big wave came along, Jason started kicking and swimming ahead of it.

"Quick! Start paddling, Amelia Bedelia!" he yelled.

Amelia Bedelia dove in front of the wave and swam with all her might. When the wave caught up to her, she pointed her toes behind her and stretched her arms out in front. She rode the wave all the way to shore, to where her parents and Aunt Mary were standing in knee-deep water.

"Nice ride, sweetie," said Aunt Mary. "You're a natural surfer girl."

"It must be the swimsuit," said Amelia Bedelia, laughing.

Her father was focused on something in the water. He reached down and plucked an object from the bottom.

"My, my, what do we have here?" he said.

He was holding a large

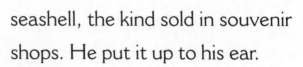

seashell, the kind sold in souvenir shops. He put it up to his ear.

"Well, I'll be," he said. "It's true—I can hear the ocean!"

"I hope so," said Amelia Bedelia's mother. "You're standing in it."

Amelia Bedelia's father held up one finger. "You want to speak to whom?" he said, talking into the shell as though it were a telephone. "She's right here." He handed the shell phone to Amelia Bedelia's mother. "Honey, it's for you."

Amelia Bedelia's mother rolled her eyes and held the shell to her ear.
"Hello, ocean?" she said.
Then a funny look came over her face.

"I hear something, but it isn't the ocean."

"Let me listen," said Amelia Bedelia. She held the shell against her ear, then threw it into the air, shrieking, *"Eeeeekkkk! Get it off me! Get it off! Get off! Gross!"*

Eeeeekkkk!!!

A baby hermit crab had latched on to Amelia Bedelia's earlobe! It hung there for a few seconds, dangling from one claw, then dropped back into the water.

They all rushed over to make sure

Amelia Bedelia was okay.

"Sorry, sweetie," said her father. "I didn't know that shell was occupied."

"Here you go," said Jason, handing the shell back to Amelia Bedelia. "You earned it. Now you won't have to buy one in a souvenir shop."

"This is the same shell?" said Amelia Bedelia. "How did you get it back?"

"I made a diving catch," said Jason.

"Next time I buy you a birthday suit," said Aunt Mary, "I'll include crab earrings."

Chapter 3
Rules of the ~~Nautical~~ Road

The sun had just peeked above the horizon. It was the crack of dawn.

"Come on, guys," said Amelia Bedelia's father. He was standing in the doorway of Jason's room. "We've got a date with a chartered party boat."

"It's too early for a party," said Amelia Bedelia,

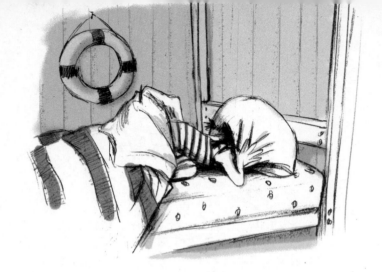

burrowing her head under her pillow.

"Way too early," muttered Jason.

"This is a fish-catching party," Amelia
Bedelia's father said. "The fish are hungry
now, and you're keeping them from their
breakfast. We'll have a whale of a time—I
promise!"

"Ugh!" said Amelia Bedelia. She
definitely did not want to catch a whale.
But she knew better than to stand
between her father and fun.

And, actually, she loved to fish too. She'd once won a bass-fishing tournament with her fishing buddy, Audrey.

They made it to the pier just in time. They raced past sailors lined up for the early-bird special at the marina diner. They rushed past a woman wearing big rubber overalls and boots and cutting up smaller fish to use for bait. As they boarded the *Reel Busy*, their fishing vessel, there was a prolonged blast from the ship's horn. It was so loud they all covered their ears.

"What was that for?" asked Jason.

"For about five seconds," said Amelia Bedelia.

"Right you are," said a gruff voice behind them. It belonged to a man barely taller than Jason. He wore a dark blue baseball cap with a huge gold anchor on the front. "Blasting the horn for four to six seconds lets everyone know we're leaving the pier. It's the rule of the road."

"We're not on a road," said Amelia Bedelia. "We're on the water."

"There are nautical rules of the road," said the man. "Ships have to obey traffic rules, just like cars. Otherwise, we'd run into each other left and right."

"You mean port and starboard," said Jason.

"Ahoy, matey," said the man. "You're saltier than you look. Follow me, and let's see what you know."

"Are we starting at the pointy end?"

asked Amelia Bedelia, pointing toward the front of the boat, where her dad was helping himself to a donut and a cup of coffee.

"Bow," said the man.

Amelia Bedelia faced him and bowed at the waist.

"Well done!" he said, laughing. "But the front of a ship is called the *bow*. The back is called the *stern*. On a ship, you

walk forward to the bow or aft to the stern. Now let's head for the bridge."

"We're heading straight for it," said Amelia Bedelia. She pointed up at the bridge that her dad had called a causeway. It was the same one they'd driven over to get to the beach. Now they were about to cruise under it.

They climbed a ladder and entered a room full of radar screens, computers, radios, knobs, and a big wheel.

"Mornin', Captain Will," said the woman standing at the wheel.

"You're the captain?" said Jason to their tour guide.

"Welcome to my bridge," said Captain

33

Will. "That's what we call the room where we pilot the ship. Have a seat, young lady."

Amelia Bedelia jumped up into the captain's chair. They were almost directly under the causeway bridge.

"Press that button for five seconds," said Captain Will, pointing at a button on the console.

BAAAAAAAAHHHHNNN!!!

The horn echoed under the bridge.

"Wow! What rule was that for?" asked Jason.

"No rule," said Captain Will, laughing. "We do that just for fun. It wakes any drivers falling asleep behind the wheel up on the bridge."

Amelia Bedelia remembered her father's reaction when the exact same thing had happened to him. Just then, he appeared on the ship's bridge.

"I've been looking all over for you two!" he said, brushing sugary crumbs from his windbreaker. "I've been up to the pointy end and back to the rear—I've been looking for you left and right."

Captain Will shook his head. "Does this landlubber belong to one of you?" he asked.

"Dad, this is Captain Will," said Amelia Bedelia.

"Welcome, sir," said Captain Will. "After you catch some big ones, these kids can take you on a tour. They could teach you a few things!"

The *Reel Busy* arrived at the fishing spot about an hour later. Captain Will

positioned his ship above some wrecked boats and old train cars that had been sunk on purpose to give fish and other sea creatures a place to live. Amelia Bedelia and Jason cast their lines and hauled in fish after fish.

"Looks like we ran into a school of fish," said Amelia Bedelia's father.

"You'd think they'd learn how not to get caught!" said Jason.

"Well, they didn't learn how to skunk us

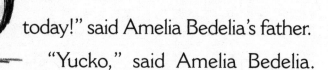

today!" said Amelia Bedelia's father.

"Yucko," said Amelia Bedelia.

She rose up on tiptoes to whisper in her father's ear.

"That's one thing I do know about boats, sweetie," he said proudly and loudly. "The bathroom is called the *head*."

A crewmember who had overheard him smiled and pointed toward a door near the stern.

"If you see a sign that says *poop deck*,

don't do it," said her father as Amelia Bedelia headed aft.

Jason burst out laughing, and said, "Only pirate ships have poop decks!"

Amelia Bedelia blushed like crazy, wondering if her father thought it was his job to embarrass her every chance he got.

As the *Reel Busy* cruised back into port, Amelia Bedelia sat with Jason and her father on the bow. It was a beautiful day, and they had plenty of fish to cook for dinner. But the breeze blowing through Amelia Bedelia's hair made her homesick for her dog, Finally. Her dog loved sticking her head out the car window into the wind. Finally would love the *Reel Busy*'s windy bow! For some reason, Amelia Bedelia blurted out, "Bow!"

"Wow!" said her father.

"Wow!" added Jason.

39

Hearing *bow-wow-wow* made her miss Finally even more. She was so busy feeling sad, she didn't notice that the *Reel Busy* was passing under the causeway bridge.

BAAAAAAAAHHHNNN!!! blared the boat's horn. They all jumped, then started laughing. They laughed all the way back to the pier.

Chapter 4

A Job for Metal Man!

One great thing about going fishing on a charter boat is that the crew cleans all the fish. Amelia Bedelia was happy not to mess around with any fish guts, and she was even happier to carry the bag of fresh fish filets home.

"What's that?" asked Aunt Mary as Amelia Bedelia tossed the bag into

Bluefish

the refrigerator.

"Tonight's dinner," said Amelia Bedelia's father. "I got some bluefish."

"My favorite color," said his wife.

"We ran into a school of fish," said Jason. "The crew said it was a fluke."

fluke

"Fluke is nice," said Aunt Mary. "Any flounder?"

flounder

"We didn't flounder at all," said Amelia Bedelia. "It was calm."

"Lovely," said Aunt Mary. "Who wants to go to the beach?"

There was still plenty of time to enjoy the beach before dinner. Amelia Bedelia and Jason carted beach towels, chairs,

buckets and shovels, a cooler full of cold drinks, and the umbrella over the dune and down to the water's edge. Amelia Bedelia's mother and Aunt Mary slathered sunblock on themselves and on Jason and Amelia Bedelia. Amelia Bedelia's father plopped down on the beach.

"Can we cover you with sand?" asked Jason.

"Be my guest," said Amelia Bedelia's father. "I could use a nap."

Amelia Bedelia's father snoozed while Jason and Amelia Bedelia got to work. Jason packed damp sand into a bucket. He turned the bucket upside down on top of Amelia Bedelia's father's stomach and then lifted the bucket straight up.

"Terrific," said Amelia Bedelia. "That looks like the tower of a castle in the Middle Ages."

"That's the idea," said Jason. He had a whole set of molds that turned Amelia Bedelia's father into a giant slumbering castle. Amelia Bedelia and Jason decorated the turrets with shells and seaweed while Amelia Bedelia's mother read her book and Aunt Mary slathered on even more sunblock and hunted for sea glass.

Amelia Bedelia's father was still snoozing when a photographer from the *Beach Gazette* took his picture.

"We'll run this picture next weekend," the photographer told Amelia Bedelia, Jason, and their mothers. "In our annual Beach Ball celebration issue."

"That will be a royal surprise for someone!" said Amelia Bedelia's mother, laughing.

It was late in the afternoon when Amelia Bedelia's father finally opened his eyes.

"Sleeping Beauty has awakened," said Amelia Bedelia's mother.

"Oh, too bad!" said Aunt Mary, shaking a bucket full of treasure. "I was just about to fill the moat with sea glass."

"Mary," said Amelia Bedelia's mother, "I didn't realize you were such a beachcomber."

"Mom, I'm pretty sure the only thing to comb on the beach is your hair," said Amelia Bedelia.

"I could be a beachcomber," said Amelia Bedelia's father, extracting himself from the sand. "Like that guy there."

They all turned to watch a man walking toward them. He was wearing headphones and carrying a short pole with a round metal disk attached to the end of it. He was slowly waving the disk over the sand from side to side, as though he was

46

vacuuming, but there was no sound.

"What's he doing?" asked Amelia Bedelia.

"That's a metal detector," said Jason. "We call him Metal Man, because he looks for stuff buried in the sand."

"What kind of stuff?" asked Amelia Bedelia.

"Any kind of metal," said her father. "Coins, keys, aluminum cans, solid gold bars . . ."

"Pirate treasure?" said Jason.

"Maybe," said Amelia Bedelia's father, patting his bathing-suit pockets. "But guys like him mainly find junk people throw away or lose. It's a weird hobby."

"Right," said Amelia Bedelia's mother.

it's not normal, like chasing a little white ball and whacking it into eighteen different holes."

"Watch it," said Mary. "I love golf too."

"I can't find my car keys," said Amelia Bedelia's father, looking back at the huge pile of sand where he had been buried.

"Sounds like a job for Metal Man!" said Jason, in a voice that sounded like he was summoning a superhero. "I'll go ask him."

Minutes later, Metal Man was waving his metal detector over the ruins of the medieval castle. He took off his headset and let Amelia Bedelia and Jason listen to the noise it made when he waved the detector over a certain crumbled turret. Amelia Bedelia grabbed a

shovel and dug out the car keys.

"I can't thank you enough, sir," her father said, reaching for his wallet.

"You don't owe me anything, glad to help," said Metal Man. "And the name is Bob Jackson."

"Ever find anything really valuable?" asked Amelia Bedelia after everyone had introduced themselves to Bob Jackson.

"A diamond ring," he said. "But I found the owner too, and gave it back.

And I found this."

Bob reached for the leather cord he was wearing around his neck and held up a coin.

"If you were a pirate," he said, "you'd recognize it. It's a gold doubloon."

"Cool!" said Jason. "For real?"

"Found it after the last hurricane," said Bob. "There just may be a whole treasure chest full of these, somewhere out there."

"Or maybe it just dropped out of a pirate's pocket," said Mary. "Like a car key."

"Yup," said Metal Man. "But you never know unless you look. And looking is the fun part."

"We'd love to thank you for

50

helping us out," said Amelia Bedelia's father. "How about dinner? We caught tons of fish today."

"Sounds like a delicious find," said Bob. "I'd be delighted."

The fish really was delicious, and so were the corn on the cob and the fresh tomatoes they got from the farm stand down the street. During dinner, Bob told stories about growing up on the shore.

"I started off as an engineer," he said. "Now I earn my living as an inventor. I get my best ideas while walking on the beach."

"Too bad you didn't invent that metal detector," said Amelia Bedelia's father. "I've seen lots of them, and I'm tempted to buy one myself."

"Oh, I did invent it," said Bob. "It's my baby. That's why I'm always on the beach, testing and improving it."

"Wow," said Jason.

"It gives me free time for travel and for fun stuff," said Bob. "This year, I'm the chairman of the Beach Ball. I hope you all can come this Saturday."

"Sure!" said Amelia Bedelia.

"Great," said Bob. "You know, when I was a kid, the legend was that this beach was discovered by a pirate looking for a place to stash his treasure."

Jason sat up straighter and taller and said, "A real pirate sailed around here?"

"So they say," said Bob. "And a half-sized replica of his ship is towed down Main Street during the Beach Ball. It's the centerpiece of the parade. You probably saw it when you drove over the bridge. The locals call the ship the *Whereami*, because the story goes that the pirate didn't know where he was."

Amelia Bedelia's mother served warm blueberry pie and vanilla ice cream for dessert, while Bob served up even more stories about the Beach Ball and about pirates. After he left, Amelia Bedelia and Jason cleared the table and helped with the dishes.

"Bob is such a nice guy," said Amelia Bedelia's mother.

"For an engineer," said her father.

"Ah, well," said Mary. "There are plenty of fish in the sea."

"Not anymore," said Amelia Bedelia. "Bob ate most of them at dinner tonight. He loved your cooking."

Amelia Bedelia's mother looked at her sister and said, "Mary, are you blushing?"

"Of course not," said Mary. "Next time I'll have to put on more sunblock."

Chapter 5

Smooth Sale-ing

Monday was not the day Aunt Mary or the weather report had predicted. Amelia Bedelia's father left between rain squalls. He was going to go to work all week and take care of Finally and the garden.

"Bye, Daddy," yelled Amelia Bedelia as he drove off through the puddles. "Kiss Finally for me!"

Back in the house, Aunt Mary was flipping her famous pancakes, and Jason was setting the breakfast table.

"Ah, well," said Mary. "It's a perfect day for sailing, spelled S-A-L-E-I-N-G. We'll cruise the outlets."

"Good," said Amelia Bedelia's mother. "You can help me find a swimsuit that's as nice as the one you found for Amelia Bedelia. Wouldn't it be fun to look like that famous painting of the goddess Venus standing on a seashell rising up from the waves?"

"That's a tall order," said Mary, serving the pancakes.

"Gee, thanks," said Amelia Bedelia's mother.

"Well," said Mary, "I bet we can find something. They say you never know unless you look."

"You sound like Metal Man," said Jason. "Only you're a bargain detector."

After Amelia Bedelia and Jason had had their fill of pancakes and bacon, Jason rolled up the runner in the hallway. He put on a pair of thick cotton socks, and he gave Amelia Bedelia a pair too.

"Follow me," he said. They sprinted across the living-room carpet to build up speed, then hit the polished hardwood floor in the hallway.

"Skimboarding without boards!" yelled Jason.

"Wheee!" screamed Amelia

Bedelia. "We're floorboarding!"

"Watch it, you two!" hollered Amelia Bedelia's mother.

Wheeee!

At last the rain let up and they all went out. Aunt Mary and Amelia Bedelia's mom took Mary's car, and Jason and Amelia Bedelia hopped on bikes and rode to town. The bikes had no gears and the tires were fat and nubby, making it easier to ride through the sand.

"Welcome to Main Street," said Jason. "It's the main drag."

"What do they drag?" asked Amelia Bedelia.

"Tourists," said Jason. "Tourists drag themselves up and down the street while everyone else drags the tourists into stores and restaurants."

"I'm a tourist, right?" said Amelia Bedelia.

"Nope, you're with me," said Jason. "I'll give you the inside scoop."

Amelia Bedelia discovered that this was true. Hanging out with Jason was like riding around with the mayor of the beach. Jason knew all the fun places to go.

Best of all, he seemed to know every kid who had a summer job. That meant they got free samples of almost everything, including candy, fudge, chowder, cotton

60

candy, caramel popcorn, ice cream, frozen yogurt, Italian ices, and smoothies.

"Hey, Captain J!" yelled a kid selling hot dogs. "You gotta try this new corn dog."

"Who is Captain J?" asked Amelia Bedelia.

"Yours truly," said Jason, taking a bite of the corn dog. "Hey, this is good! Try it, Amelia Bedelia."

Amelia Bedelia looked around to make sure there weren't any dogs watching, then took a bite.

"Best corn dog I've ever eaten," said Amelia Bedelia. Which was true, since it was the only one she had ever

eaten. They washed down the corn dog with a free fresh-squeezed lemonade at the Beachcomber Diner, their next stop.

Later they ducked into Seaside Pets to chat with a kid who knew all about saltwater aquariums. A parrot named Flint kept squawking, "Pieces of eight, C.J.! Pieces of eight, C.J."

Amelia Bedelia couldn't believe it. Even the parrots seemed to know her cousin!

"You have a million friends, Captain J," said Amelia Bedelia. "Summer must be really fun."

"Yup," said Jason. "We surf a lot. The only problem is the tourists."

"Aren't tourists just

people on vacation?" asked Amelia Bedelia.

"That's true," said Jason. "Most are nice, but some drive me and my friends crazy."

Riding back toward the house, Amelia Bedelia and Jason passed a bathing-suit shop. Amelia Bedelia skidded to a stop. The mannequin in the window wearing a bathing suit looked just like her mother. The mannequin waved to her.

"Mom!" yelled Amelia Bedelia. They parked their bikes and ran inside.

"What have you

two been up to?" asked Amelia Bedelia's mother. "Hang on, I'll get dressed and we'll head for home."

"Send your Pearl over tomorrow," said Aunt Mary to the saleswoman as they left.

"What Pearl?" asked Amelia Bedelia.

"Did you buy another ring?" said Jason.

"It's a surprise for you two," said Mary.

"Cool," said Jason. "What's for dinner?"

"That depends," said Mary. "What are you and Amelia Bedelia making for us? Your aunt and I are on vacation."

"I know!" said Amelia Bedelia. "Let's make reservations. How about that pizza place we passed?"

"Perfect!" said Jason. "We haven't been

there yet—I know a kid
who works there."

"My Jason likes to have his fingers in a lot of pies," said Mary.

"And Amelia Bedelia makes amazing lemon tarts," said her mother.

"They're small," said Amelia Bedelia. "Just big enough for one finger."

The delicious pizza dinner, the cool rainy weather, the yummy snacks and samples, and biking around all day made Amelia Bedelia sleepier than usual. That night she lay on the bottom bunk listening to Jason read his favorite book—*Treasure Island*—out loud to her.

Amelia Bedelia still loved being read to,

and the words filled her head with images of pirates, sailing, and the sea. She must have dozed off, because the next thing she knew, the lights were out.

Amelia Bedelia was sure that she was dreaming when she saw Jason climbing down the bunk-bed ladder. She drifted in and out of sleep as he rummaged around in the closet. She was almost sure she saw him tiptoe to the window, lift the screen, and slip outside.

With her eyes half shut, Amelia Bedelia groggily dragged herself out of bed and staggered to the window. A bike disappeared into the darkness. Flopping back into bed, she concluded that she must be dreaming. Why else would

Jason be dressed like a pirate?

"Hey, Captain J," she called out. "No more reading *Treasure Island* before bed." She waited for him to answer but fell asleep before he did.

Chapter 6

Pearl Comes Out
of Her Shell

The next morning, Jason was impossible to pry out of bed. The only thing that worked was the aroma of his mother's waffles. As she served him a second helping, Aunt Mary made an announcement.

"Jason," she said. "Guess what? You know how, every

summer, you bug me for sailing lessons? Well, the woman who helped us in the store yesterday told us that her daughter has her own sailboat and sometimes teaches kids to sail. Do you know her? I signed you two up . . . apparently she's shy, but once she starts talking about boats, she comes out of her shell."

Amelia Bedelia was wary. The last thing that had come out of its shell had clamped on to her ear. "I hope she isn't crabby," said Amelia Bedelia to her waffles. This girl must be tiny if she could fit into a shell. Was her sailboat tiny too? Like the one she had seen inside a bottle at the souvenir shop?

Just then there was a knock at the door. "Jason," said Aunt Mary on her way to answer it. "Your ship has come in."

"Boat," said Jason. "Sailboat."

A girl with a long blond ponytail ambled into the kitchen. She was older than Jason, and a lot taller too.

"Pleased to meet you," she said, staring at the floor. "I'm Pearl."

"Have a seat, Pearl," said Mary, setting another waffle on the table. "So,

your mom says you're an expert sailor."

"I was born on a sailboat," said Pearl, digging into her waffle.

"I'd love to live on a boat," said Jason.

"Have you guys ever been on one?" asked Pearl.

Jason shrugged and said, "We know better than to call the front the pointy end."

"That's a start," said Pearl, smiling. "At least you won't have any bad habits to break."

After breakfast, Pearl, Amelia Bedelia, and Jason hopped on their bikes and

headed to the marina where Pearl docked her boat. The boat was a beauty, built of real wood with shiny brass fittings.

"*Mother-and-Father-of-Pearl*?" said Jason, laughing. "That's the name of your boat?"

"I had to give my parents credit," said Pearl. "This boat was a wreck when they bought it for me, but I managed to fix it up, and now I keep it shipshape."

As they put on life jackets, Amelia Bedelia wondered what other shape a ship would be.

Carshape?
Planeshape?
Dogshape?

Pearl untied the lines holding her boat to the

pier. She showed Jason how to hoist the sails. When a breeze filled the sails, they began moving out into the bay.

"What makes a sailboat sail?" asked Pearl.

"That's easy," said Amelia Bedelia. "Wind blows against the sails."

"And that pushes the boat through the water," added Jason.

"Right," said Pearl. "That works as

long as the wind is blowing in the direction you want to go, like now. But how are we going to get back? What if you need to go where the wind is blowing *from*?"

Amelia Bedelia looked at Jason. He didn't have a clue either. They shrugged.

"Don't we have to wait for the wind to change directions?" asked Jason.

"You could," said Pearl. "Or you could turn toward the wind and adjust the sails to take advantage of it. Sails are simply giant vertical wings, like on an airplane. The force in front of the sail actually drags the boat forward through the water instead of pushing it from behind."

Pearl grabbed a notebook and drew a sketch to show them how a sail works.

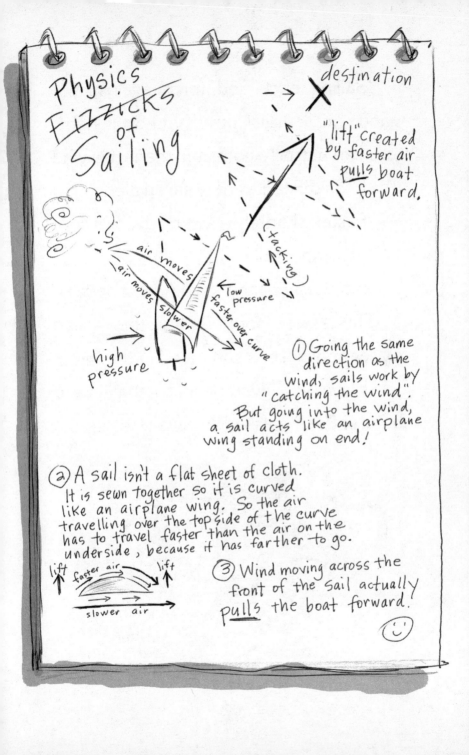

Physics
~~Fizzicks~~
of
Sailing

destination

"lift" created
by faster air
pulls boat
forward.

(tacking)

air moves
air moves slower
faster over curve
low pressure

high
pressure

① Going the same
direction as the
wind, sails work by
"catching the wind".
But going into the wind,
a sail acts like an airplane
wing standing on end!

② A sail isn't a flat sheet of cloth.
It is sewn together so it is curved
like an airplane wing. So the air
travelling over the top side of the curve
has to travel faster than the air on the
underside, because it has farther to go.

lift   faster air   lift
slower air

③ Wind moving across the
front of the sail actually
pulls the boat forward!

☺

"Sailing back and forth against the wind is called *tacking*. If you do it right, you can actually go faster than the wind itself," said Pearl as they sailed along.

"Faster than the wind?" said Jason. "That's impossible."

"No, that's science," said Amelia Bedelia.

The lessons continued as they sailed closer and closer to an island in the bay.

"Have you ever been to that island before, Pearl?" asked Amelia Bedelia.

"Nope," said Pearl. "I've sailed around it in races, but I've never bothered to go ashore. Funny how you don't usually do things right on your front doorstep."

"Or on your starboard side," said Amelia Bedelia.

"Very good," said Pearl. "You'll be a sailor in no time."

Pearl pushed the tiller over and steered closer to the island for a better look.

Jason stood up. "LAND—*WHOA!*" The sailboat ran aground with a jolt, tossing him off the bow and into shallow water.

"Man overboard!" yelled Pearl.

"Where?" yelled Amelia Bedelia. "I only see Jason!"

"I'm okay," Jason called back. It was so shallow, he could stand.

"It's a sandbar," said Pearl. "Sorry—but Jason, no standing up while sailing. If the wind had shifted, the sail would have swung around. You could have been hit by the boom and knocked out."

"He *was* knocked out," said Amelia Bedelia. "Knocked out of the boat."

"True," said Pearl, as she lowered the sails and dropped the anchor to keep the boat from drifting away. Then they waded ashore. The beach was covered with seaweed and driftwood and shells. The island was overgrown with bushes and vines. They could hear birds chirping.

They found a narrow path and followed it to an old cottage. The roof sagged, but the sturdy walls were still standing.

"Knock, knock. Anyone home?" Jason rapped on the front door. The door creaked on its hinges, then slowly fell into

the house with a crash.

"I hope there are no rats or bats or snakes in here," Jason said. He walked into the cottage, into what must have once been the living room. Amelia Bedelia and Pearl were right behind him.

"If you're trying to scare me," said Pearl, "it won't work."

They stood close together, letting their

eyes adjust to the gloom. The room had floor-to-ceiling windows on three sides, but the glass was missing. Tall bushes growing outside had begun to reach into the house.

"Hey, what's in those bushes?" asked Jason. Now they could see hundreds, maybe thousands, of black, shiny, beady eyes. Amelia Bedelia, Jason, and Pearl froze, like small birds under the spell of a snake. Thousands of eyes stared back at them, unblinking.

"If you're trying to scare *me*," said Amelia Bedelia, "it's working."

Chapter 7

Berried Treasure

As her eyes adjusted to the dim light, Amelia Bedelia tiptoed cautiously across the cottage floor. In slow motion, she thrust her hand into the leaves, into the center of a shiny black cluster. She carefully pulled out a handful of what looked like beady eyes.

"Yum, blackberries!" she said, popping one into her mouth.

Blackberry bushes had surrounded the house, growing up to the roof and creeping in at every window.

Amelia Bedelia picked another handful and passed the berries to Jason and Pearl.

"They're amazing," said Pearl.

"Yeah," said Jason, stuffing berries into his mouth. "There must be millions. We're rich."

They ate their fill and then some. Pearl even ran back to the boat, grabbed a bucket, and they filled that too.

"If we need tons of blackberries, we know where to come," said Amelia Bedelia.

"Blackberry Island," said Jason and Pearl.

"Weigh the anchor, Amelia Bedelia," said Pearl when they were back on the *Mother-and-Father-of-Pearl*.

Amelia Bedelia lifted the anchor. "About twenty-five pounds," she grunted.

Pearl smiled. "Exactly right," she said.

It took all three of them to shove the boat off the sandbar and into deeper water.

"Hoist the sails," called out Pearl.

"Aye, aye, Captain Pearl," said Jason.

Wind filled their sails with a pop.

Pearl steered as they practiced

tacking on their way back to the marina.

At the beach house, they found Amelia Bedelia's mother and aunt sipping iced tea and studying cookbooks.

"The Beach Ball committee assigned me dessert," explained Aunt Mary. "And I'm supposed to bring a giant one."

"You're a great baker," said Amelia Bedelia's mother. "Your fruit cobbler would . . . "

"Would cost me a fortune," said Mary. "I'd need tons of fresh fruit."

Amelia Bedelia and Jason looked at each other, then at the bucket of blackberries they had brought back from the island.

"Try some of these," said Amelia Bedelia.

Her aunt and mother marveled at the size and flavor of the berries.

"There are lots more where those came from," said Jason. "How many buckets do you need?"

After dinner, Amelia Bedelia and Jason played board games while their mothers played cards. Amelia Bedelia could hardly keep her eyes open. She was glad to finally climb into bed, but she was having so much fun! Her dad would have loved sailing with Pearl.

In the cozy bedroom, Jason began reading his favorite part of *Treasure Island*

to Amelia Bedelia. She was super tired, but she was also determined to stay awake this time, in case Jason really did go out the window.

Finally Jason turned out the light.

"Hey, Amelia Bedelia," said Jason.

She was awake, but she did not answer.

"Amelia Bedelia?" said Jason, once more.

Amelia Bedelia kept her eyes shut and listened to the crickets. She kept her eyes closed as Jason tiptoed down the ladder, changed clothes in the closet, and snuck

out through the window.

Amelia Bedelia leaped out of bed and dressed in a flash. She climbed out the window, got on her bike, and began pedaling like mad. Soon she spotted Jason up ahead.

Amelia Bedelia was going so fast that she almost ran into another bike crossing the road. She skidded to a stop and came face-to-face with Pearl.

"Amelia Bedelia?" said Pearl. "What are you doing? Why are you out so late?"

There was no time to explain. "Please, Pearl, come with me," gasped Amelia Bedelia. "I'm worried about Jason."

"What's Jason doing?" asked Pearl.

"I don't know," said Amelia Bedelia. "He went thataway."

They took off together after Jason. Amelia Bedelia was pedaling furiously. She was furious at Jason. Why was he sneaking out at night, all by himself?

They followed him down a narrow sandy path with tall grass on either side. Pearl and Amelia Bedelia set down their bikes and crawled to the top of a dune,

where they could see everything. A campfire was roaring, surrounded by about twenty boys dressed like pirates.

Amelia Bedelia recognized most of the pirates. Jason had introduced her to them. By day, these boys worked at the shops, food stands, and restaurants on the main drag. But where was Jason?

 "Check out those tattoos, gold earrings, and eye patches," whispered Pearl.

"And the skulls and crossbones," whispered Amelia Bedelia.

Just then the boys knelt down

together as someone wearing a large coat with gold buttons approached the campfire.

"Jason!" Amelia Bedelia blurted out.

Pearl clamped her hand over Amelia Bedelia's mouth and pulled her down behind some beach grass. A few of the boys turned around but did not spot them.

Amelia Bedelia could not believe her eyes. Her cousin Jason was a pirate!

Chapter 8

X Marks the Spot

Jason—*Captain* Jason—stood on a milk crate to address his crew of pirates.

"Shipmates, this Saturday night, every landlubber on this beach will have to reckon with us!"

"Har! Har! Har!" hollered the crew.

"The Beach Ball will be a soggy bust!" yelled Jason.

"Arrr! Arrr!" hollered the crew.

Captain Jason made an X in the sand with a plastic cutlass. "Shipmates," he said, "X marks the spot. When the float of the *Whereami* sails into the intersection of Main and Pier Streets, we strike! Navigator, report!"

"Aye, aye, Captain Jason," said the kid from the hot-dog stand. "I'll hoist the Jolly Roger when the float is on the X."

"Avast!" said Jason. "Gunner, report!"

The kid from the pet store put a model ship in the middle of the X. Then he turned to the crowd. "That ship will get a

Aye! Aye! Aye!

tye!

Aye, Aye! Aye! Aye!

broadside of forty beach balls filled
with water," he said. He lifted one of the
balls and tossed it high in the air. It landed
with a *BWOOOSH!*, spraying
a tidal wave of water that
swept the ship model away.

BWOOOSH!

"Jolly job, matey," said Jason. "Wait
until I give the order to fire. Then hurl the
beach balls at will."

"Aye, aye, Captain," said the gunner.

At Will? wondered Amelia Bedelia.
Wasn't he the captain of their fishing-
party boat?

"Cookie, report!" said Jason.

The kid who worked at the cookie shop
stepped forward. "In the
confusion,

me and my men will raid the dessert table and bring the goods back here."

"Bravo!" said Captain Jason. "After Saturday night, every landlubber will know once and for all who runs this beach."

"We do!" shouted the crew of pirates.

"The Beach Ball!" said Captain Jason. "If you can't beat it, sink it!"

Amelia Bedelia and Pearl watched as the pirates started dancing around, giving one another high fives.

"Yo-ho!" they shouted, then began chanting. "Sink the float, sink the float, SINK THE FLOAT!"

Out of the pitch darkness, something swooped down and landed on Amelia Bedelia's shoulder. She squealed, "What is it? Pearl, help!"

"Shhhh! Quiet," said Pearl. "Oh, my gosh. It's Flint, that parrot from the pet store."

"Pieces of eight! Pieces of eight!" squawked Flint. "Come and get 'em! Come and get 'em!"

Crawling on their bellies, the girls barely made it back to their bikes before the pirates overran their hiding spot.

On the ride back home, they talked about what they had seen and began wondering what they could do about it.

Chapter 9

Suit Yourself

When Amelia Bedelia woke up the next morning, Jason was still sound asleep. Amelia Bedelia was not surprised. She went into the kitchen.

"Morning, sweetie," said her mom, handing her the phone. "Talk to Dad."

"How's the surfing life?" asked her father. The connection was bad, and Amelia Bedelia could hardly hear him.

"Great!" said Amelia Bedelia. "I started with a skimboard, and Jason said he'd teach me to boogie board. Next I'll be on a surfboard."

"Sounds like you've been completely bored," said her father.

"Oh, Daddy," said Amelia Bedelia. "I've been sailing too."

"Checking out the sales with mom and Aunt Mary?" said her father.

"No," said Amelia Bedelia. "Hoisting sails with Jason and Pearl."

"Pearl?" said her father. "Is Mom

buying jewelry? Put her back on."

"He wants to talk to you again," said Amelia Bedelia, handing the phone back.

Amelia Bedelia was eating a warm blackberry muffin when Jason entered the kitchen, dressed and ready to go, like last night had never happened. She couldn't believe it.

After breakfast, Amelia Bedelia, Jason, and Pearl sailed back to Blackberry Island. They'd brought along plenty of pails and buckets to hold the berries Aunt Mary needed. Jason and Amelia Bedelia took turns at the tiller. Pearl was working on her tan. "We make a good crew," she said.

Once they had arrived at the island and

anchored the boat in a calm spot, they jumped overboard and waded to shore. It was sunny and hot, a perfect day for picking blackberries. They had twenty empty pails, which they filled as quickly as possible, racing one another.

"Ouch!" said Amelia Bedelia.

"Watch those thorns," said Pearl. "They're like sharks' teeth."

"Only sharper!" said Jason.

After they had loaded the full pails

onto the *Mother-and-Father-of-Pearl*, they headed back to the marina with Pearl at the tiller.

Jason gestured to the mainland. "Arrrrgggghhhhh! Let's sack the city and head for the bounding main!" he yelled.

"Spoken like a true pirate," said Pearl.

"I'd love to be a pirate," said Jason.

Pearl looked at Amelia Bedelia. "Even if someone got hurt?" she asked.

"I'd never hurt anyone," said Jason.

"What if someone's feelings got hurt?" asked Amelia Bedelia.

"Or a whole town's feelings?" asked Pearl.

"Feelings! That's all girls worry about," said Jason. "That's probably why there were no girl pirates."

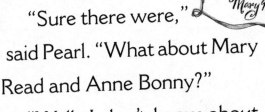

"Sure there were," said Pearl. "What about Mary Read and Anne Bonny?"

"Well, I don't know about them, but I'd never have a girl in my crew," said Jason, standing up to adjust his swimsuit.

"It's lucky for you I don't feel that way about boys," said Pearl. "You'd have to swim home."

Just as Pearl spoke, the wind shifted, swinging the boom across the boat and

knocking Jason out, into the bay.

"Man overboard!" yelled Amelia Bedelia. Pearl pushed the tiller over hard. The boat came back around. Amelia Bedelia looked for Jason, but the only sign of him was his bathing suit floating on the waves. Then Jason's life jacket popped him up, sputtering and coughing, to the surface. Pearl retrieved his suit with a boat hook and dangled it just out of his reach.

"Give me my suit!" yelled Jason.

"Did you forget?" said Pearl. "I'm a girl. I may not *feel* like it. But speaking of feelings . . . how will people at the Beach Ball feel when you ruin the parade and soak them with water?"

Jason glared at the two of them.

"Who told you?" said Jason. He was

treading water.

Amelia Bedelia looked at him. "You did," she said. "I was worried about you sneaking out at night. We followed you and overheard your plans for the Beach Ball."

"Are you going to tell?" asked Jason.

"We probably should," said Pearl.

"You're being really mean," said Amelia Bedelia.

"We'll make a deal with you," said Pearl. "Promise us you won't hurt anyone."

"Feelings *or* bodies," said Amelia Bedelia.

"Just think about what you are doing and how it affects others," said Pearl. "Just remember, we are all in the same boat."

"Okay," said Jason. "It's a deal."

He snatched his suit, put it on, and climbed into the boat. No one said a word the whole way home.

A familiar face was waiting for Amelia Bedelia on the pier. Her father was back for the long weekend, and he had brought along a surprise visitor.

"Finally!" Amelia Bedelia called out.

Finally pulled and pulled at her leash until she got free. She raced along the pier, jumped off, and swam for their boat.

Amelia Bedelia scooped her onboard, laughing when Finally nibbled her on the chin. Then Finally began shaking off so much water that Pearl said, "One more shake and she'll sink us."

"Yeah, Finally," said Jason. "We're all in the same boat."

Chapter 10

One Last Normal Day

Amelia Bedelia's father helped them carry the buckets of berries back to the house.

"Welcome back, honey!" said Amelia Bedelia's mother. "You're a celebrity." She held up a copy of the *Beach Gazette*. Amelia Bedelia's father had made the front page. His face was sticking out of the sand castle that Amelia Bedelia and Jason had built on top of him while he slept. The headline read A MAN IS HIS CASTLE.

Amelia Bedelia's father shook his head. "The saying is 'A man's home is his castle,'" he said.

"But in this case you *are* the castle, dear," said Amelia Bedelia's mother. "My Prince Charming, with your head in the sand."

"Like an ostrich," said Amelia Bedelia.

"Hey," said her father. "Isn't anyone happy to see me?"

Amelia Bedelia and her parents shared a family hug while Aunt Mary admired the buckets of berries.

"We can quadruple the recipe," she said. "I've got a deep ceramic pan that's perfect for cobbler." She took off her rings and started making the dough. "We'll bake it now and heat it up tomorrow. That intensifies the flavor."

Pearl and Jason began by washing the berries.

"I have an idea," said Aunt Mary.

"Amelia Bedelia, do you remember how to make a mud pie?"

"Yuck!" said Amelia Bedelia. "I haven't made mud pies since I was little. If you're serving blackberry cobbler, who'd want a pie made of mud?"

Aunt Mary laughed. "Amelia Bedelia, I think your mother needs to teach you about mud pie!"

Amelia Bedelia's mother smiled and got out her recipe for mud pie.

"Anything with this much chocolate has to be good," said Pearl, reading it over.

"Let's each make one," said Amelia

Bedelia. "We can call it Pirate Pie."

"Good idea," said Pearl. "We can cut each pie into eight pieces."

Then Jason had an idea. "Call it Piece of Eight Pie, like the money that pirates used. We can get chocolate coins from the candy shop, and you can put one on each slice."

They all got on their bikes to go downtown to the candy store. Amelia Bedelia was happy that things felt normal again, if only for one more day.

Chapter 11

How to Bake a Clam

It was the day of the Beach Ball. Bob Jackson showed up on the doorstep bright and early with a bunch of buckets and shovels.

"Let me guess," said Mary. "You hit the jackpot and need our help digging it up."

"I wish," said Bob. "No, it's my job to dig a hole on the beach and build a fire

to cook the seafood for tonight's feast. I thought the kids would like to learn how to make a clambake."

"Absolutely!" said Amelia Bedelia's mother. "Take my husband along and teach him too."

Amelia Bedelia shook her head. "Does it take this many people to bake one little clam?" she asked.

hard shell clam

They all piled into Bob's pickup and rode down to the beach. The tide was out, and Bob showed them how to look for little bubbles on the mudflats. He dug down less than a foot and scooped out a clam.

"We call this a steamer," he said, holding it up. "Amelia Bedelia, let's see if you and Jason can fill these buckets

Steamer
clam

with clams while your dad and I go down to the marina for the rest of the seafood."

Amelia Bedelia picked up the steamer. When she turned it on its side, it looked like an old steamboat. "Toot-toot!" she said, wiggling the steamer at Jason. The clam shot out a little stream of seawater.

"Ahhh!" she yelped, and dropped it back in the bucket.

Amelia Bedelia and Jason took turns spotting air bubbles and digging up clams. They learned that if they stamped on the sand they could sometimes make a clam shoot up water. They had filled two buckets by the time her father and Bob got back.

The bed of Bob's truck now held large tubs full of live creatures in seawater. Some

tubs were full of waxy cardboard cartons, surrounded by crushed ice. Amelia Bedelia's father passed out breakfast sandwiches while Bob drew a diagram in the sand and explained how to construct a clambake.

"I don't even think I like clams," said Amelia Bedelia.

"That's okay," said Bob. "There's more to a clambake than clams. A clambake is just

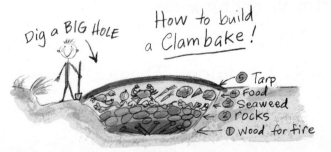

Dig a BIG HOLE

How to build a Clambake!

⑤ Tarp
④ Food
③ Seaweed
② rocks
① Wood for fire

a way to cook with steam on the beach. We add sausages, potatoes, onions, carrots, and corn on the cob too. For the main course, we'll have lobsters, crabs, quahog clams, littleneck clams, and the steamers you two dug. And plenty of mussels."

"Good," said Amelia Bedelia. "Because my muscles are already aching."

"Do you have enough energy left to help me dig the pit?" asked Bob, handing her a shovel.

While Amelia Bedelia and Jason dug a deep pit in the sand, Bob and Amelia Bedelia's father collected large round stones that reminded her of cannonballs.

"First we'll build a fire to heat up these rocks," said Bob. "Then we'll sweep off

the fire and cover the hot rocks with wet seaweed. Next, we'll pop the food on the steaming seaweed, then cover the whole thing with a tarp to keep the steam in. That's how the food cooks."

They gathered buckets of wet seaweed and left them next to the pit. "All set," said Bob. "Later today, my second clambake crew will arrive and start cooking. They're experts at tending the fire. You're in for a tasty treat."

Bob dropped them back at Mary's house.

"You know, my great-uncle was a chef on a cruise ship," said Amelia Bedelia's father. "I have his recipe for clam chowder. It's always a big hit at our family reunions."

"Why don't you enter the

chowder competition?" said Bob. "We have plenty of clams." He grabbed a bag of fresh clams from the truck and gave it to Amelia Bedelia's father. "Good luck," Bob said. "Thanks for your help."

Amelia Bedelia's father roped Amelia Bedelia and Jason into chopping, slicing, and dicing the onions and celery and carrots and potatoes while he cleaned and cooked the clams. Amelia Bedelia did not like clams, but the aroma of her father's chowder was changing her mind. She might have to try a spoonful.

Chapter 12

Fighting Fire with "Fire!"

As the Beach Ball festivities got underway, Amelia Bedelia and Jason sat on the porch. They watched tourists walking by, wearing all kinds of crazy costumes. Jason was dressed like a pirate again.

Bob arrived to pick up the desserts and chowder. When they went inside, Amelia Bedelia found her father relaxing

in the kitchen, wearing a combination lock on a chain around his neck.

"Guess who I am?" he said.

They all shrugged and shook their heads.

"Ever hear of Davy Jones's locker?" he asked. "Well, I'm his locker partner."

"Oh, Daddy," said Amelia Bedelia, "that is so embarrassing."

"I think it's nice and simple," said Bob. Then he produced his costume. "It's the tradition for the guy in charge to wear this getup," he said. He had traded in his metal detector and baseball cap for a trident and a crown.

"You'll make a fine King Neptune," said Amelia Bedelia's father.

Amelia Bedelia's mother and Aunt Mary appeared at the kitchen door. Amelia Bedelia's mother was wearing a shiny green bathing suit and a long skirt covered in green sequins. She looked like a mermaid.

Aunt Mary wore a big wig with long golden curls covering her bathing suit. She'd borrowed Jason's skimboard and decorated it to look like a shell. When she stood on it, everyone was speechless.

"Mary, you did it!" said Amelia Bedelia's mother. "You look just like the painting."

"You look like Queen Neptune," said Amelia Bedelia.

"Wow," said Bob. He just stood there, gazing at Mary. "Wow."

"Jason," said Aunt Mary, "you may want to change. I think every boy passing by the house today is dressed like a pirate."

"Not just the boys," said Pearl. She'd been at the front door. Now she walked in, flourishing a long, curved plastic sword. She looked pretty fearsome. "Pirate Pearl, at your service," she said, curtsying.

"Nice tattoo," said Jason, admiring the bleeding-skull transfer on her forearm.

"I've got a pirate outfit for you too, Amelia Bedelia," said Pearl, winking at her. "If you can't beat 'em, join 'em. We can be Pirate Pearl and Admiral Amelia Bedelia."

"Aye, aye," said Amelia Bedelia, grabbing her art supplies so they could add final touches to their costumes. Amelia Bedelia even made a shark fin out of cardboard for Finally and strapped it around Finally's furry belly. Amelia Bedelia's pirate costume came with an eye patch. She drew an open eye on it and put it on.

"That looks so weird," said Jason.

Then Amelia Bedelia attached two seashells to a headband. When she put it on, the seashells dangled by her ears. "These are my ocean stereo headphones," she said. "When I want to hear the ocean, I hold them up to my ears."

Jason laughed. "Hermit crabs not included, I hope."

"Amelia Bedelia, you'd make an awesome inventor," said Pearl. "Like Bob."

Amelia Bedelia, Jason, and Pearl left Aunt Mary's house and joined the crowd of people streaming downtown. Bob left at the same time. He was off to deliver the food, then hook the *Whereami* float to his truck and tow it to the clambake.

Amelia Bedelia was feeling uneasy, thinking about the surprise the pirates had in store for all these tourists and hoping Jason was going to do something about it. When they got to the intersection of Main Street and Pier, Jason stopped.

"One of my friends works in this building," he said. "He invited me up on the roof to watch the parade. You can come up too, if you want."

When they got to the top, Amelia Bedelia and Pearl saw boys dressed as pirates hiding on every rooftop as far as the eye could see. Amelia Bedelia also spotted plastic milk crates loaded with

beach balls full of water. Amelia Bedelia
wondered when Jason was going to stop
the sacking of the city!

Meanwhile, the good ship *Whereami* was
"floating" down Main Street behind Bob's
pickup truck. The streets were crowded,
and the turn onto Pier Street was tight.
And that was when it happened.

A gust of wind caught the pirate flag on the *Whereami*, furling it against the glowing cone of one of those tall outdoor gas heaters that restaurants use to warm customers who sit outside at night. The flag smoked for a second, then burst into flames.

"Fire!" hollered someone in the crowd below.

Jason glared at the other pirates. "Who said that?" he demanded. "I didn't give the order to fire!"

A chorus of voices arose from the street. "Fire. Fire! FIRE!!!"

Amelia Bedelia and Pearl ran to the edge of the roof. The

130

burning flag was setting the sails on fire.

"Fire!" yelled Pearl.

"What are you doing?" yelled Jason.

Amelia Bedelia lifted up her eye patch and studied the scene below. She could see that only one thing would stop this fire—water.

Then Jason ran to the edge of the roof. "Oh, no!" he said.

"Jason," said Amelia Bedelia, "you need to fire."

A look came over Jason's face. All of a

sudden, he knew just what to do. Pointing his cutlass at the blazing *Whereami*, he hollered, "FIRE!" As soon as he did, every pirate unleashed a beach ball on the ship.

BOOOSH! BOOOOSH! BAH-BOOSH!!!

Beach ball after beach ball sailed through the air and hit the good ship *Whereami*. The balls exploded, and water soaked the sails and the deck. The fire was out!

Everyone down on the street began clapping and cheering.

"Bravo!"

"Go, pirates!"

"Shiver me timbers!"

The pirates on the rooftops waved down at the crowd.

Pearl began laughing. "Everyone thinks that you guys are the fire department," she said. "You're heroes!"

Jason shook his head. "What do they know?" he said. "Tourists—ha!" But now he was smiling at Pearl and Amelia Bedelia.

Chapter 13

Another Job for Metal Man

The clambake was a huge hit. There was plenty of food for all. Everyone agreed that this was the best Beach Ball ever. The desserts were arranged on a table decorated to look like an island, complete with a tiny palm tree and a sign that read DESSERT ISLAND.

Mary's cobbler even had a sign that

said BERRIED TREASURE next to it. People
were lining up for a taste, but she hadn't
served a slice. She looked worried.

"Anything wrong?" asked Bob.

"Well, after I made the cobbler, I
couldn't find my favorite ring," she said.
"I hope it didn't get baked into the cobbler.

I don't want to tear the whole cobbler apart looking for it, but I don't want anyone to choke on it, either."

"Serve the other desserts," said Bob. "I'll be back."

The last sliver of Piece of Eight Pie was being served when Bob returned with his metal detector. He waved it over the cobbler.

"Hey, it's Metal Man!" said someone in the crowd.

"Lose your fortune in the dessert?" asked someone else.

"King Neptune gets first choice," said Bob, pointing at a particular section of cobbler. "Cut me a slice right there."

As Mary did, there was a *clink*. Bob pulled her ring

out of his piece of cobbler.

He wiped off the ring and placed it back on Mary's finger. Mary blushed.

"You keep forgetting to use sunblock, Mary," said Amelia Bedelia's mother, laughing. "There may be plenty of fish in the sea, but there's only one King Neptune."

"You mean Metal Man!" said Amelia Bedelia.

Bob thumped his trident on the table, and the crowd quieted down.

"I'd like to thank all of you who made this Beach Ball possible," he said. "Thanks for your tasty food and hard work. Tonight, when I looked in the rearview mirror of my truck, I saw that I was being followed by a pirate ship on fire. I asked myself the same question that first pirate who landed here probably asked . . . WHERE AM I?

"But then Long John Jason and his pirate crew came to the rescue and put out the fire. That's when I knew exactly where I was. I am on the best beach, with the best friends ever."

Bob paused because people were clapping and hooting. He motioned for Jason to join him. When the applause died

down, Bob continued, "Jason, you not only saved the Beach Ball, you made it the most exciting Beach Ball ever. In recognition, I'm presenting you with this doubloon that your pirate ancestor long ago probably left here for you to find." Everyone cheered again as Bob took the doubloon from his own neck and put it around Jason's.

Later, when Amelia Bedelia, Jason, Pearl, and an assortment of pirates were eating mud pie down by the water's edge, Amelia Bedelia bumped Jason on the shoulder. "Cousins are the best, matey!" she said.

Chapter 14

She Smells Seashells

When their week at the beach was over
and they were finally back home, the first
thing that Amelia Bedelia unpacked was
the shell that Jason had saved for her. She
kept it on her nightstand. She loved the
difference between its dull, rough outside
and the smooth, shiny pink inside.

Whenever she needed to take a break to

BAAAAAAAAHHHNNN!

get away from everything, Amelia Bedelia would close her eyes and hold that shell up to her ear. She could hear the ocean, of course. But she also heard the sounds and voices of her week at the beach. She heard . . .

The *BAAAAAAAAAHHHHNNN!!!* of the fishing boat's horn under the causeway.

Her father snoring as they covered him with sand.

The metal detector beeping when it located metal.

The *thwap* of sails filling with wind.

Jason yelling, "Fire!"

The *booosh!* of a beach ball bursting on the *Whereami.*

Cheers and clapping for Jason and his pirates.

141

Amelia Bedelia could even smell the smells of the beach. The salt air, the sea, her father's prize-winning clam chowder (which she had tasted and loved), the clambake, and the world's best blackberry cobbler, bubbling and baking.

Aunt Mary had sent them a copy of the *Beach Gazette* with the write-up of the Beach Ball. The picture on the front page showed the smoldering pirate ship. But the article also featured a picture of Amelia Bedelia's father under the headline FESTIVAL CROWNS "CHOWDERHEAD." That clipping held a place of honor on their refrigerator for months.

FESTIVAL
CROWNS
"CHOWDER-
HEAD" my
hero.

Her mother had written "My hero!" above it.

Thanks to her cousin Jason, Amelia Bedelia's dreams were now filled with pirate adventures. She would sometimes wake up from a sound sleep convinced that Flint the parrot had just swooped down on her, squawking, "Pieces of eight, pieces of eight!"

Then Amelia Bedelia would put her shell to her ear and let the ocean rock her back to sleep.

143

Amelia Bedelia's Mud Pie ♥

Ingredients

2 cups graham cracker crumbs

6 tablespoons unsalted butter (melted)

¼ cup sugar

3 ounces semi-sweet chocolate chips (plus extra for decorating)

¼ cup sweetened condensed milk

1 cup cold milk

1 package instant chocolate pudding mix

4 ounces whipped topping (optional)

Directions

1. In a small bowl, combine graham cracker crumbs with butter and sugar, and stir until mixed well.

2. Press the mixture against the bottom and sides of a 9-inch pie pan until completely covered. You can use your fingers or a spoon.

3. Put chocolate chips in a microwave-safe bowl and heat for thirty seconds at full power.

4. Mix the sweetened condensed milk into the softened chocolate chips and stir until smooth. Pour the mixture on top of the graham cracker crust and spread evenly with a spoon or spatula.

5. In a large bowl, combine the cup of milk and the pudding mix, whisking or stirring with a fork until smooth. Set aside for 3 minutes, or until pudding has started to set.

6. Pour the pudding into the crust on top of the chocolate chip layer.

7. Chill the mud pie in the refrigerator for three hours, until it's completely set.

8. Decorate the mud pie with whipped topping and chocolate chips, if you want to. (You can buy whipped topping or make your own by beating whipping cream until it's stiff.)

Then cut and serve!

Two Ways to Say It

By Amelia Bedelia

"Have a whale of a time!"

"Have a big, exciting time!"

"The last one in is a rotten egg!"

"Run fast— and don't be last!"

"Let's go beachcombing."

"Let's search the beach for shells and treasures."

"I'm going to catch some z's."

"I'm going to get some sleep."

"We were skunked."

"We couldn't do what we planned."

"I'll meet you on the main drag."

"I'll meet you on the busiest street in town."

"I keep it shipshape."

"I keep it super clean and organized."

"I'll give you the inside scoop."

"I'll tell you what really happened."

"She has her head in the sand."

"She is clueless!"

"He has his fingers in a lot of pies."

"He does a lot."

With Amelia Bedelia

#1

Amelia Bedelia wants a new bike—a brand-new shiny, beautiful, fast bike just like Suzanne's new bike. Amelia Bedelia's dad says that a bike like that is really expensive and will cost an arm and a leg. Amelia Bedelia doesn't want to give away one of her arms and one of her legs. She'll need both arms to steer her new bike, and both legs to pedal it.

Amelia Bedelia is going to get a puppy—a sweet, adorable, loyal, friendly puppy! When her parents ask her what kind of dog she'd like, Amelia Bedelia doesn't know what to say. There are hundreds and thousands of dogs in the world, maybe even millions!

#2

Amelia Bedelia is hitting the road. Where is she going? It's a surprise! But one thing is certain. Amelia Bedelia and her mom and dad will try new things (like fishing), they'll eat a lot of pizza (yum), and Amelia Bedelia will meet a new friend—a friend she'll never, *ever* forget.

anything can happen!

#4

Amelia Bedelia has an amazing idea! She is going to design and build a zoo in her backyard. Better yet, she is going to invite all her friends to bring their pets and help plan the exhibits and rides.

Amelia Bedelia usually loves recess. One day, though, she doesn't get picked for a team and she begins to have second thoughts about sports. What's so great about racing and jumping and catching, anyway?

#5

#6

Amelia Bedelia and her friends are determined to find a cool clubhouse, maybe even a tree house, for their new club. One day they find the perfect spot—an empty lot with a giant tree. The lot is a mess, so they pitch in and clean it up. And that's when the trouble really begins.

The Amelia Bedelia Chapter Books
Have you read them all?

Coming soon!

Coming soon!